MAGGIE'S DAY OUT

Illustrations by

Jan Lewis

DEAN

We're going to the zoo today!
Mum, Jim, Charlie, Nick and me, Maggie.

"I want to see tigers!" says Charlie.
"I want to see kangaroos!" says Nick.

I spy, I spy, with my little eye,
Lots of different things outside.

Nick doesn't like long car journeys.
He turns a funny colour, so we open the window.

Charlie wants us to see the chimpanzees.
"Oooh!" go the chimps, swinging from
branch to branch.

oooh

"I wish I could climb trees like that!" says Nick.
"They can use their feet like hands,"
Mum tells him.

I like the pink flamingos best. They can stand on one leg.

"The scorpions have a sting in their tail," says Jim.
"They sting the locusts and then they eat them."

"Let's have locust sandwiches!"
shouts Charlie.

Rumble, rumble, rumble goes my tummy.

My banana sandwich is yummy.
Charlie can't finish his sausage.

Look at the lion's big teeth. I wonder how
many sausages he can eat?

Nick and I want to be kangaroos.

Charlie looks just like a little tiger.

The camel's humps are swaying to and fro! Charlie and Nick are shouting.

Jim carries me. I think he's much
better than a real camel.

Time to go home,
time to go home.

Smile everyone!
Going to the zoo is lots of fun.

BIG TEETH

Illustrations by

Jan Lewis

Today we have an appointment at the dentist.
"Let's clean your teeth before we go," says Mum.

Squirt, goes the toothpaste onto the brush.
It's got blue and white swirls and tastes like mint.

We get to the dentist early and have to wait.

But what's this?
An animal with really BIG teeth!

"Hello, Nick and Maggie and Charlie," says our dentist. "You've grown since the last time I saw you!"

There's a funny smell, but the dentist says it smells that way because it's clean.

"I don't want to go first!" Nick says. I sit with him in the big chair so he won't be scared.

"It's like a ride at the fun fair!" Nick smiles.
The dentist puts on a mask and switches on
a very bright light.

"I see a wobbly tooth," says the dentist
as she looks inside Nick's mouth.
"Soon your milk teeth will fall out."

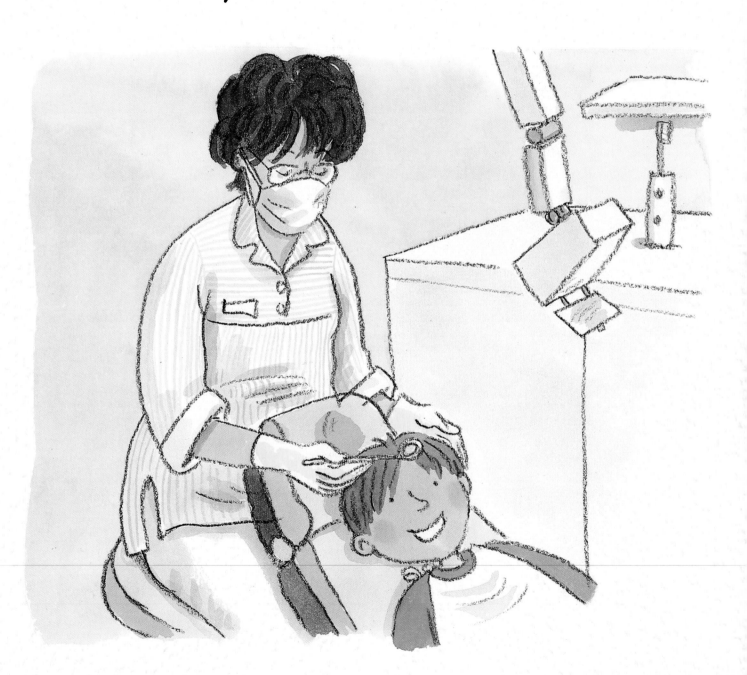

My teeth aren't loose at all!
"Your milk teeth will fall out when you are as
old as Joe," says the dentist. "Then new ones will
grow and stay for a long time."

Charlie doesn't have wobbly teeth yet either.
But the dentist sees something else. She sees a
little hole in Charlie's tooth.

"We have to fill this little hole so it doesn't get bigger," the dentist says to Charlie. "What happens if it gets bigger?" he asks.

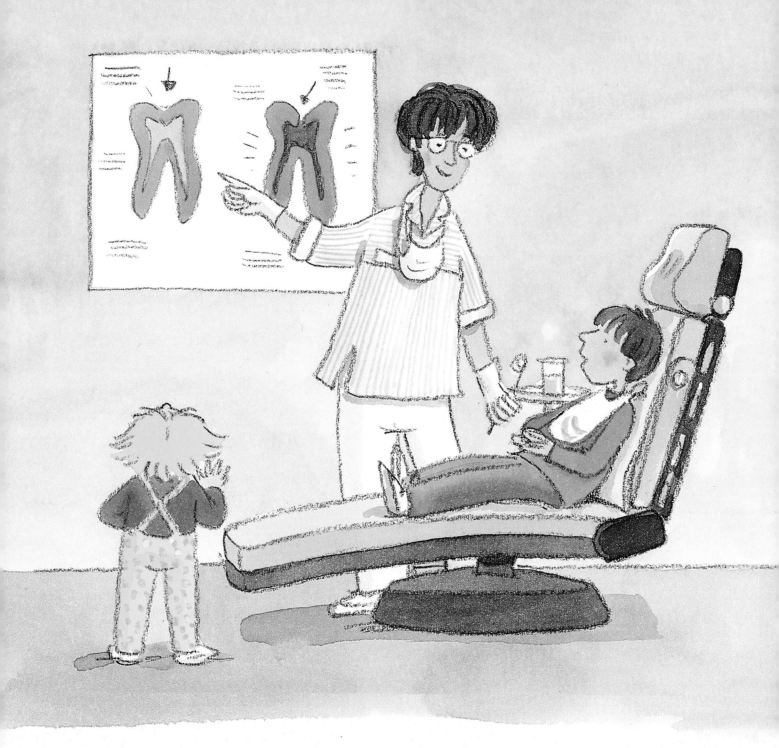

"It could turn into toothache," she explains.
"So I'll need to use the whizzy drill and fill
the hole with a filling."

It doesn't take long before Charlie's tooth
is filled. "That didn't hurt at all," Charlie says.

Now one of Charlie's teeth has a shiny silver bit!
Charlie shows it off to me and Nick.

I want my teeth to stay white!
"Be sure to brush them twice a day, and they will,"
promises the dentist.

Smile!

Bye-bye, Mr Crocodile!
We'll see you next time.